THIS
HOSTEL
LIFE

Melatu Uche Okorie

D1355022

Skein Press
2018

A CIP catalogue record for this title is available from the British Library.

First published in 2018 by
Skein Press
skeinpress@gmail.com

ISBN 978-1-78808-491-8

Cover design: Alan Keogh
Typesetting: Mariel Deegan
Printed in Dublin by SPRINTprint Ltd

www.skeinpress.com

For Josephine Useinatu, may she rest in peace.

CONTENTS

Author's Note

The state of affairs in ******direct provision hostel: 28/03/2013 00:51

*For years, the direct provision hostel based in ****** has been acknowledged as the best maintained direct provision hostel in Ireland. However, this hostel has changed drastically in recent times and everyone has turned a blind eye to it. Residents are now mainly asylum seekers who were transferred from other hostels. For this new set of residents, having a bit of privacy makes up for all other issues they had to face in their previous hostels and thus, they are unwilling to complain over the way things are run here. Most have probably protested against the management in their former hostels and are hesitant about being labelled troublesome here. But direct provision is like being in an abusive relationship. Abuse in itself is homogenous,* *no matter what race, class, or in this case, the hostel of the abused.*

****** is made up of rules that are almost Machiavellian, inane in nature. You never know what you're going to wake up to each morning. It's either that the management has given the order that the quantity of washing powder for each resident will be reduced to half of the white plastic cup or an essential provision has been withdrawn.

The worst hit is the dining room. The lunch, which was usually served between 12–2 p.m., was changed to 12–1.30 p.m. while dinner, which was usually served between 5–7 p.m., was moved to 4.30–5.30 p.m. We swallowed it, as the management knew we would, even after we had complained and they had promised to 'look into it', the recurrent answer.

I, like other residents, have learnt to live under these almost tyrannical conditions. After all, no one would like to be moved as the devil you know is always better than the angel you don't. Apart from the arbitrary changes to our daily routine, the security men also try to intimidate residents like myself who they know will complain about the food options. I would usually find two of them standing directly behind me whenever I'm *in the queue for food. It became obvious to me that it was a way of breaking my spirit more than anything else. There are tons of cameras in ******, but I would find these security men trailing after me, sometimes, as I walk to my room. I was ready to endure the intimidating and bullying behavior of some of the security men and the condescending tone of some of the staff, however, my frustration has grown so much in the past few weeks, I stopped going to the dining room in the evenings. I tried hiding away in my room and buying my own food just to avoid seeing them, but with a child and €28.70 as weekly money, I could not sustain that.*

I came to Ireland from Nigeria twelve years ago. Everything about my life in Nigeria, my upbringing and why I came to Ireland is all in my stories. I find it easier to talk about myself that way. I'm not a natural sharer. I'm really thankful to God that I've found, in writing, a medium through which I can comfortably talk about myself. At first, I was very grateful for a safe space to lay my head, a bed, a roof over my head, anonymity. All of that, I was very grateful for. But as with everything in life, needs change and the place you once regarded as a safe haven can soon start to feel restrictive. I spent eight and a half years in direct provision. In May of

2014 I got 'leave to remain', and as I held the letter in my hand, I felt fear. I asked myself 'is this it?' Living in direct provision was the only life I had known since coming to Ireland, so I was genuinely scared.

Since leaving direct provision, life has been a struggle. I think there should be more support for women parenting alone and, perhaps, immigration flexibility for grandparents and other family members to visit Ireland to see their loved ones. A lot of women parenting alone, especially those without family support in Ireland, are struggling mentally, financially and emotionally. This family group is often ostracised in society and can experience intimidation and condemnation. Generally, Ireland could benefit greatly from people becoming kinder towards each other.

Sometime in 2007, not long after I was put into a direct provision hostel, I told my friend, Audrey Crawford, who was working for Spirasi at the time that stories were running around in my head. Her response was simple, 'write them down'. I can't remember if I acted on her advice immediately, or perhaps I was encouraged to do so after she handed me an ad for a writing competition. But, what I do remember is staying up all night to write two stories: 'Gathering Thoughts' about a young girl who underwent female circumcision and 'Matters of the Heart' about two lovers breaking up. Audrey loved 'Gathering Thoughts' so I sent it to the competition, unedited and with plenty of grammatical errors. I shiver to think about it now. Despite its roughness, 'Gathering Thoughts' was still chosen as the winning story, while 'Matters of the Heart' remains unpublished to this day (my last attempt at writing a romance!).

Before hearing of the success of 'Gathering Thoughts', I started to write more. I loved the fact that I was writing things that my friends could read. Every movie I watched and every soap opera on television became a story prompt. You can tell this from the titles I gave them: 'My Chemical Brother', 'A Good Turn', 'London Bridge', 'A Price Too High'. I had yet to learn to draw from things that were happening in my day-to-day life. But the well for those sorts of stories soon dried up. I was beginning to feel the isolation of living under direct provision. My child was growing up with me as her only family.

As much as I was trying not to let it show on the outside, I was hurting desperately on the inside.

Memories of home birthed new stories. It wasn't a conscious thing. One of the stories I wrote at that time was 'The Egg Broke' (in this collection). This story is about the killing of twins, an old practice that was abolished sometime in the mid-1900s after religion was introduced to my village. The idea came from what I could remember of an old tale my mother had told me as a child. It was about a woman whose twins were killed due to the practice. She was pregnant a second time, and when she and her husband realised she was carrying twins again, they ran away from the village in the middle of the night. The last that was heard of them was that they had joined a church.

Another shift came in my writing. This time it was brought about by some changes that were happening within the direct provision system. As the impact of the economic crash in Ireland was beginning to be felt, stricter immigration rules were introduced and deportations were escalated. Women, men and children were taken away from their direct provision hostels in the middle of the night and deported. I remember waking up one morning to find my next door neighbour's room empty. There were all kinds of stories about what happened to my neighbour and her family. Some said she and her three children were deported, others said they ran away to Dublin, Belfast or Canada. To this day, I can still recollect my child, who was two and a half years old at the time, running to our neighbour's door, sometimes pressing the door handle in a bid to open it, other times just pausing as if listening for someone before running back to me. This happened for nearly two weeks. My daughter was too young to put into words what she was seeking. There was also a lot of fear at this time, a lot of sadness, separation, pain, discontent and anger. Apart from the deportations, there were also the transfers between the direct provision hostels. Residents were being randomly transferred from one hostel to another. The managers of hostels became powerful as residents became more afraid and paranoid.

The changes and moods of that period influenced the stories that I call the Asylum Series. One of the lighter pieces from this series is 'This Hostel Life' (in this collection). I told the story from the point of view of a Congolese woman for whom I created a language, a mixture of Nigerian pidgin English and some American slang words which she speaks in a strong Kinsala accent. The idea was born from my observation of how the different nationalities in the direct provision hostel were reconstructing language in order to communicate with one another. The Nigerian pidgin English (albeit with all kinds of variation) became one of the most commonly spoken, which is not surprising as Nigerians made up the highest number of residents.

Even though 'Under the Awning' is set outside of the direct provision system, I wanted to highlight the everyday racism that most African people living in Ireland who I've had conversations with have faced. The idea of making it a story within a story happened serendipitously. I was once part of a writers' group and had presented what I call the main story at a workshop. The feedback I got was that the story was too dark and harsh. As I was replaying in my head the comments I got in the feedback, and doodling them down, the idea came to me to frame the main story around the feedback.

The stories in this collection represent a part of my life since coming to Ireland. They not only touch on emotions and feelings that have affected me over those years, but also helped put them into words. I have been helped and encouraged by many and I am forever grateful. May God bless you all.

Melatu Uche Okorie
20 December, 2017

This Hostel Life

10:26 a.m.

From the window, me I can see everybody is here, and me I can see the place is also full. Mercy voice reach my ear before me I even go inside.

'Mehn,' she say, 'that grey hair really freaked me out this morning.'

And me I hear everybody laugh. Dis make me start to think if dey are talk about old age, and where Mercy see grey hair because she no too old like dat.

I use my back to push open the door because I hol buggy for my hand and the door is too heavy to open with my hand and hol the buggy at the same time. I am still try for turn around and face everybody when I hear my neighbour, Franca, shout, 'Yee! Look, who is here.'

'Craa-zy!' My friend Ngozi voice boom as she hail me and start to wave for me to come stand with her. I start to pass all the people and all the buggy, holing my own buggy.

'Too many people is here today, Mama,' I say to Ngozi when I finally reach her side. 'Me I hope you get number for me.'

Then I start to hug everybody; Mercy, her friend, Mama Bomboy, Mummy Dayo, Franca.

'Ah, you know today is Monday naw, they won't let me collect number for someone who is not here.' Ngozi voice match her size. She is a big woman and her voice is big and sound like man voice. She like to call everybody 'Crazy' and I have hear some Nigerias complain behind her back dat their name is not 'Crazy,' and their Mama is not call them 'Crazy' and dey will tell her dat the very next time she try to call them 'Crazy'. Me I don't mind that she call me 'Crazy', I must tell you. But you know all dis Nigerias, dey like to fight all the time.

Me I am here for collect my provision and toilet-tings for dis week. We collect only for Mondays and Tuesdays for the dining room in dis hostel. Dat is why there is many humans and buggies.

The first time my husband see me carry buggy like dis, he say, 'Dis woman, why you carry buggy and you don have baby inside?'

'Dat is what everybody do here!' me I tell him.

But dat is before. Now, if he ask me dat type of question again, me I'm gonna say to him: 'How you gonna know what everybody do when you sit inside all time for watch football?'

* * *

In my last hostel, dey give you provision any day, but it's gonna be one month since you collect last. So if you get toilet paper today, it's gonna be one month before you get another. Dat is why me I happy when dey give me every week for here, but now, me I don feel happy again. Dis direct provision business is all the same, you see, because even if you collect provision for every week or you collect for every month, it is still somebody dat is give you the provision. Nothing is better than when you decide something for yourself.

But me I still like dis hostel more than my last hostel. Because here, we have one big room, and inside, me I use one corner for make small my own kitchen, and we get bathroom and toilet for inside the room, and my husband and me we have our own bed and my two daughters have their own bed too. Before, all of us use common toilet and bathroom and common room. Dat's why me I don like to complain too much for this hostel like some Nigerias.

Just last week, me I see Mummy Dayo outside her house on my way to laundry. She was stand with Franca talking. Me I greet Mummy Dayo, and say, 'Mummy Dayo, you no collect provision today?' Me I don't like for talk to Franca too much because she do things to make me to be angry.

'I no dey bother myself to dey waka about on Mondays, *o jare*. From here to there, from there to here, for what!' She answer me like she angry.

'Me too,' Franca quick quick say. She like to agree for everything everybody say.

'From laundry to collect provision, from collect provision to check laundry, from check laundry to see GP, from see GP to collect food, from collect food to check laundry.' Mummy Dayo start to count for her finger. 'Up and down, up and down from morning till evening!'

Mummy Dayo is a small woman like dis, but she talk fight fight all the time. Me I know her now, but before, if I see her talking to somebody and shaking her head dat she always tie with scarf, I use to think she's gonna fight dem. Even now, she is roll her eyes and look me up and down as she is talk. 'I just do the things I can do and leave the rest for God.'

Me I agree Monday morning is crazy crazy for dis hostel because everybody like to go collect provision and toilet-tings. But you can go for Tuesday and they tell you, 'We've run out of toiletries!', and dat's the end.

Everybody like to see GP for Monday too. Dey say the GP for Monday is better than the GP for Tuesday because he give better medicine. And sometimes, when you go to see GP, you remember dat you need to see social for something because dey share the same building and those social people can put up sign anytime changing the time dey for see people. And as you do all of dis, you are washing clothes for the laundry too because you don want to leave dirty clothes for house from weekend.

Sometimes, I tell myself, it is not good to do everything for Monday because you stay like dis, nothing to do, for all the other days but it is not good to start week lazy too.

'Who is give number?' I ask Ngozi. She is my close Nigeria friend and me I like her very much. She talk free free like me and does not care about anybody. People tell me before, when I first come this hostel: 'Be careful of Nigerias; do not make friends with Nigerias; Nigerias like to make trouble and fight too much; the management don't like Nigerias.'

It's not like dat for my last hostel where everybody do everything together. But me I still listen, and I go close to my own people, and make friends with only Congolese people and go only Congolese party. But now, me I know no one is good complete and no one can do you bad like your own people. So me I start to make friends with Nigerias again. And if dey do me bad, I show them I don come Europe to take shit from anybody. Now, dey laugh and say, 'Beverléé, you're crazy,' and dey make my hair for free and give me good price for sew my clothes. Now, all Congolese people come to me and start to say, 'Please Beverlée,' for connect dem to my Nigeria friends.

Mercy is one for answer me. She point for some place behind Ngozi and say to me, 'You better go quickly and get your number. Then come back and I will tell you where I see grey hair for my body this morning.'

Everybody laugh again. I look behind Ngozi and see one man. He is wear the uniform for the hostel security.

'I never see dat man before,' me I say.

'He new, my sister,' Mummy Dayo tell me for sad voice and shake her head like something disappoint her. 'I speak to am. He from one of those fake *oyinbo* country. Meee, I don't really like all those people! They racist pass Irish!' She look for where the man is stand holing something for his hand and hiss.

Ngozi laugh and push Mummy Dayo shoulder small. 'This woman,' she say, 'you're too funny.'

Mercy look Mummy Dayo with no laugh for her face. She has tell me before dat Mummy Dayo is too old to be talking the way she talk.

Me I look at the man again and he look me and look away. Maybe he can tell we are talk about him. Even though I don like the way Mummy Dayo look the man like fight, I don say anything to her. Me I know Mummy Dayo don like anybody and always say something about everybody:

'Those Moslems, me I suspect dem too much o. I no follow dem do anything.'

'Dat Cameroon girl, she can like to do *shakara*. I no know who she think she be.'

'Congo? Dey crazy pass Nigeria o! We Nigerias, na only mouth we get, but Congo fit take knife fight you.'

'Eastern Europeans dem all be fake *oyinbo*.'

'Irish people too dey cold. Whisper, whisper, all the time.'

She have warn me about Ngozi many times. She say, 'Be very careful. Igbo people na real scorpion. If you stop to watch dem for one minute, anything you see, you have to take it like that. I like you, that is why I am telling you all dis things.'

She even warn me for women from Franca kind of country, Zimbabwe, Kenya, Uganda, South Africa and she tell me, 'You better watch your husband around those women. Their toto loose like anything.'

But from everybody, me I know she hate Benin more. I know this because she don like Mercy. She say, 'Benin people na the real best for everything.

Dem be best liar, best criminal, best prostitute, best husband-snatcher.' As she is tell me dis, she is count her finger, 'all the bad bad things for this world, na dem be best for them. No let anybody you know marry Benin. Me, I be Nigeria, dat is why I know all dis things.'

Me I leave Ngozi and the other women to go get ticket for collect provision. One, two, three, four people have reach the security man before me, so I wait for him to tear ticket one by one to give everybody. He no say anything to anyone. He just tear ticket and give, tear ticket and give. The ticket is small like this, like the one you get when you want to do raffle. It reach my turn and he tear ticket and give me. Me I look my number, it is 126.

Just then, the woman who give provision come out from the office where she give provision and stand for the door. She is wearing white coat, like the type the nurses wear for hospital and me I can hear the sound of keys jiggle for inside the pocket of her coat. She is a fat woman like dis and the manager for the dining room. She don say anything to the new security but it look like he fear small to see her stand like dat. He look the ticket book for his hand and start to call out numbers quick quick. He is a very tall man and look like he can even be the father for the manager for the dining room.

'Number eighteen? Number eighteen?'

I no know why, but me I just start to feel sorry for the security man. I can see he no shout very well for the people to hear him, so me I start to help him to shout.

'Number aaeeteen! Number aaeeteen!' I shout loud and loud because the noise for the dining room is too much and many people are talking for small small group. Soon, other people start to join me to shout the number.

'Number aaeeteeeen! Number aaeeteeeen!'

The next thing me I see is the manager waving for the security man to come and I stop to shout to see what she gonna do. The security man go for where she stand. He bend him head like dis because the noise is much. The manager say small thing to him dat me I cannot hear before she turn and go back inside the office. It look from her face like she no happy with the new security man and the way everybody is shout. The security man fold the ticket book for him hand and put it for him coat pocket and he stop to shout 'number aaeeteen' with us.

Just then, one small group of people start to clap. One man is start to walk to a window where he gonna collect provision. He has his hand up for air like this, holing the number eighteen ticket. He is a Somali man. He is wear glasses and is smiling like someone has catch him doing something dat is not good and he is sorry for dat. Quick, I look Mummy Dayo and she is look the Somali man up and down like dis as he walk pass her, and after he pass her, she turn and say something for the other women and everybody laugh. As soon as I see dis, me I hurry to go for join dem.

'Honest to God, naw, that is what I heard.' I hear Ngozi say when I come back with my ticket.

'How you know it's true?' Mercy is ask her.

'Ah, ah, I hear the girl say it on the television with my own ears, naw!' Ngozi say like she is start to vex with Mercy small. She raise her hand which hol her ticket and shake it for me to show it is near her turn to collect provision and she leave.

'Most of my references these days are from reality television, too.' Mercy friend, Mama Bomboy, say with gentle voice like she is try to make peace.

'No be only you, my dear sister,' Mummy Dayo cross her arms for her chest and sigh. 'How man for do? No work, no nothing. Na only television person dey watch every time.'

'Try to understand me,' Mercy say, touching Mama Bomboy for arm. 'Why is Ngozi saying something she hear from television like she hear it from the doctor?'

'What the matter?' me I ask Mercy. 'You talk about the grey hair?'

'Ah beg, make we no talk about that grey hair matter again,' Mummy Dayo say, shaking her head.

'Ngozi just told us that she heard from a woman on the *Real Housewives* that eating yam helps with fertility.' Mama Bomboy is the one to answer me. 'You know that show, don't you?' she ask me with worry face.

'Oh, me I know the show,' I answer Mama Bomboy. I like her very much because she talk different from everybody. 'But I don watch it all the time. I don understand all the things for there.'

'Ah, me too o! The kin' English dey speak, me I don't understand at all,' Mummy Dayo say and hiss.

Mama Bomboy look Mercy quick, like she is sorry for what Mummy Dayo is saying. Ngozi has tell me many times dat Mama Bomboy no get confident and dat her husband bully her for house. But me I no agree with Ngozi. Mama Bomboy is gentle and she respect people and she no like to fight. Beside of dat, me I can tell dat Mama Bomboy go correct school, so me I don think any man can bully her.

'But what dat mean? Fertility?' I ask Mama Bomboy.

Mama Bomboy wait small, like she want to make sure Mercy is not gonna talk before she start to answer me. 'Fertility means a woman can have a baby, I think.' She look for Mercy again like she want to see if Mercy want to say something but Mercy no look her.

'Aeh, so Ngozi know this yam for help woman get baby and she no tell me? And she know me I am try to find boy baby for my husband.'

'How is Ngozi suppose to know you want to have baby at your age!' Franca shout for me and dat make me angry. She always like to talk like she know something but me I know she just pretend.

'No, no, no, Mama,' me I shout back for Franca. 'Why me can't have baby for my age? What wrong for that?'

'You see what I mean?' Mercy say, holing me for shoulder like she want me to stop to be angry. 'Beverlée has bought into the yam story without asking question.'

'Aeh, the woman for television no eat the yam?'

Mercy put her other hand for her mouth like dis, like she want to use the hand to stop the laugh from come out, but her shoulder is shake small small.

'See Beverlée,' she say after small time, 'not everyone on the television knows what they're talking about.'

'The television is our modern-day pop culture,' Mama Bomboy say and smile for me.

Me I smile back for her. I no understand her what she mean but me I just like way she talk.

'Do you know that same woman on *Real Housewives*, yeah?' Mercy stop to look all of us for face one by one like she want to tell us something big. 'She said they have 265 days in a year.'

'OMG! Imagine that!' Franca shout, like what Mercy talk is real bad something. She like for act like small girl sometime, and for copy Mercy and Mama Bomboy because Mercy have live for London before and Mama Bomboy speak correct English. Mummy Dayo has tell me that Franca is forty-four years old like me just dat she no get children and she no get husband, and when woman no get children or no get husband, it is hard for tell her age. And that is why me I try not to be friends with Franca because me I have to be careful for my husband.

'How many days it suppose be?' Mummy Dayo ask Franca the question for my mind.

'It should be 365,' Mama Bomboy is the one for answer her.

'Or 366, depending …,' Mercy say and Mama Bomboy nod her head quick like dis.

'Why it depend?' me I ask and look Franca straight.

Me I want to see if she even know the answer the way she shout 'OMG' but she no look me at all. She just keep her head down like dis, like she busy for something.

'February is sometimes 29 days,' Mama Bomboy is the one to answer me again.

'Na true, na true,' Mummy Dayo say and nod her head as she twist her mouth. Dis make me start to think for my head dat maybe she is tired of dis television talk. Me too I am begin to tire of the television talk.

'Do you know?' Mercy say again, like she just remember something. 'I think that same woman in *Real Housewives* has never heard of Gandhi.'

'Who dat?' me I ask her. 'All dis name we don't have for Congo.'

'Na one man!' Mummy Dayo answer me quick as she use her shoulder to push my own. She no want me to continue the television talk with Mercy.

'What of that boy in *Big Brother*, what's his name again? He has never heard of Shakespeare!' Mercy say, looking at everybody but everybody look back at Mercy quiet. Mummy Dayo roll her eyes and start to tap her foot. Me I can see she is now real tired for Mercy talk.

'What?!'

Ngozi shout make all of us for jump. She is back from collect provision and she is carry a big Lidl bag. A man who is stand near for us move away. He is not happy for the shout.

'Which kind stupid boy be that?' Ngozi say. 'You no hear of Shakespeare for Congo, Beverlée?' she ask me.

'Aeh, it's long time me I hear about this Shakespeare man for Congo, looong time for Congo.'

Everybody start to talk for same time about Shakespeare, except for Mummy Dayo. She is busy for look inside Ngozi Lidl bag, and she is count all the provision inside. Me I have to say dat I look small, and me I see two box for Rice Krispies, two box for Cornflakes, one packet for sugar, one packet for Lyons tea. Me I cannot see the things under but me I can see that Mummy Dayo is try to see dat. Maybe she want to know if Ngozi is get more provision than she. Me I know some people come for dining room just to see what provision dis person or dat person collect, and after that, dey gonna use it for fight staff. Me I have complain about dis to Ngozi, but she see it different. She say why staff not give everybody the same because everybody for equal. She say to give some persons special things is quick way for cause trouble for a place like dis.

'Guess what?' Ngozi say, 'My husband say he was watching one programme …'

Mercy raise her hand for Ngozi to stop. All of us quiet and listen. The security man have start to shout another ticket number. Everybody look their hand but for all of us, nobody is hol the number.

'I better go,' Mercy point for her ticket. 'It soon be my turn.'

'Eh-ehe, like I was saying,' Ngozi start her story again. 'My husband was watching this programme …'

'Dis provision number just dey move slow slow.' Mummy Dayo is the one for stop what Ngozi is talk about dis time.

'What you expect?' Franca say in her small voice, pointing for the provision window. 'Only two people is serving.'

Me I follow Franca hand and see dat only the manager and one staff is stand for window. Nobody is there for the other two provision windows.

'Only two people is serve all dis number of people?' Me I shout for surprise.

'Dem dey outside dey smoke,' Mummy Dayo nod her head like she is know many things we don know. 'After dat, dem go take break. Dat's Irish people for you!'

'But why waste person time for here?' Me I ask with small anger. 'Me I get laundry to go after this provision.'

'My husband say one nineteen-year-old boy did not know his alphabets,' Ngozi start her story again. But me I am not listen to her because me I have many things I am gonna do dis morning and she is finish for collect her provision.

'Nineteen years old!' Ngozi continue for her story, shaking her head like the thing she talk about is hard for her to understand. 'And my husband say the presenters were laughing. They thought it was funny.'

When I see nobody is answer Ngozi, me I start to feel small bad for her.

All dis children for here, they don know nothing, Mama,' me I tell her.

'They are crazy!' Ngozi say and laugh.

'Dey real crazy, Mama,' I say and join her for laugh.

Just then, Ngozi see one man holing a jar of honey coming from provision window. She turn for look me. 'Ehen, Beverlée,' she say, 'I forget to collect something. I'm coming,' and she hurry back to the provision office window. Mercy is also stand for the provision window. Me I see Ngozi say something for Mercy and Mercy shift aside for her. The staff come for the window and me I see Ngozi tell her something. She look down for the paper for her front and tell Ngozi something. Then Ngozi say something back for her.

'Who do you think you are?' me I hear the staff shout for Ngozi. As everybody hear the staff shout for Ngozi, everybody is quiet, and start to listen. Even Mercy is look at Ngozi like she wait for her answer to the question.

'And who do you think you are too?' Ngozi is ask back and she is point at the staff as she is talk. Me I see the manager leave her window and come for the window where Ngozi and the staff is stand and argue.

'Is Ngozi fighting?' Franca ask like all of us are no seeing the same thing.

'Listen Ngozi, we are not allowed to give honey to anyone,' the manager tell Ngozi like she not in the mood for too much talk.

'Then why did she give that man honey just now when I ask for it first? This is what you people do all the time! You always pick people you want to give this or that. Why?' Ngozi voice is loud now as she is talk.

The new security man come and stand for the back of Ngozi but he no say or do anything. That make me I know he really new. The other securities will hol and carry anybody they see for argue with staff.

'Well, that is the last honey we have and we've just given it out,' the manager answer Ngozi in a way everybody can tell she is lying but there is nothing Ngozi can do about it.

'You better find one for me o, because I'm not leaving this place until I get one.' Ngozi tell her and fold her hands. Me I wait to hear what the manager gonna say to Ngozi but she just move back. She push away the paper where people for sign their name for provision out of the way, then she take one side of the window and close it. She do the same for the other side of the window too.

Ngozi run to the second window but the manager come there and close dat window too. Then she and the staff come out of the provision office and she take the bunch of key for her coat pocket and start to lock the door.

As soon as all the people see dis, dey start to shout. 'You can't just lock up because of one person. We've been waiting here for long. What do you mean?'

But the manager no say anything to anybody. Dis make all the people angry more and dey start to shout for Ngozi.

'If there's no honey, why not take sugar?

'Is sugar and honey not the same thing?'

'All these women that like to make trouble.'

12:01 p.m.

Small small, all the people have start to go as dey see the manager is not gonna change her mind and open the office to give provision. Mercy and Mama Bomboy, then Franca and Mama Dayo, all go. Now me I can see new people have start to line up outside the dining room for lunch. I take my empty buggy and open the dining room door. I am quiet and sad as I go. Ngozi is my best friend for dis hostel but I have to leave her. From the window outside, me I can still see her stand alone for the dining room, fighting for her honey.

Under the Awning

Everyone was already in as she had hoped. She sat on the first empty chair she saw, and when she had finished arranging herself – getting her pen and papers out, making sure her phone was switched off, zipping up her bag – she finally looked up and realised she was sitting directly opposite the leader. The large window behind him was slightly open. Outside, the weather was as unsettled as her disposition as if it was ruminating on whether to rain or not. The sun had also not bothered to come out, leaving the sky an unpleasant grey.

Today was her turn to present her work at the writers' group. The leader took a sip out of a paper cup on the table in front of him.

'Can you read us into your work?' he asked the girl, placing the cup back on the table.

'Where would you like me to start?' she replied, hoping he would want an extract only as he sometimes did.

'Why don't you read it all?' he said, looking enquiringly around the room like the thought had just occurred to him.

She bent her head and started to read, stuttering her words.

You stood under the awning outside the Spar shop, staring straight ahead, barely moving, a pink plastic folder tucked under your arm, waiting for the drizzle to stop. You felt uncomfortable not standing at the bus stop on the edge of the pavement because you knew that back home, life would not stop over 'this small rain'. The newspaper vendors would still blow their whistles in your face, with The Guardian, The News, *and* The National Enquirer *flapping in a transparent plastic bag on their arms. The hawkers would still walk around with trays on their heads, calling out 'Buy* Akamu! *Fresh corn with fresh coconut!* Agege *bread!' The blind beggars with plates in one hand and the other tucked into the hands of their small guides would still approach cars in traffic, singing blessings in pidgin English, Igbo, Hausa and Yoruba.*

Back home, rainfall meant other things to you rather than discomfort. It meant that the flat you shared with your mother's sister and her husband and your three cousins would not be stuffy. It meant that you wouldn't go to the well to fill the jelly-cans in the flat with water. It meant that there would be corn sellers lined up along your street selling your favourite fresh roast corn the next morning.

But here you were desperate not to stand out, so you stood with the young woman pushing a crying toddler in a stroller, and the two older women and an old man under the awning of the Spar shop, careful not to look directly at anyone, pretending not to be paying attention. You had observed it was the way of things here, so people were not made to feel uncomfortable, even though you could hear the woman with the stroller pleading with her wailing child to stop throwing her toys out of her pram, and the two women and the old man talking about the weather.

You got on your bus and after a while it filled up but the seat next to you remained empty although there were people standing in the small aisle. You stared out of the window, willing the bus to move faster. A few stops later, you felt someone sit beside you. It was a white-skinned woman, but when her phone rang, she answered in a language that was not English.

You got off at your stop and you immediately searched out the house with the little children who always shouted 'Blackie!' at you, but there was no one at the balcony, so you hurried past with relief.

You walked into the house in which you lived with your mother and your two siblings and saw your mother's friend, Aunty Muna, sitting on the sofa in the living room. 'Good Afternoon, Aunty,' you said, and she laughed, 'Haw haw haw,' before saying you were becoming the only African teenager she knew in the country who still said good afternoon and not hello. Her loud chortle made you remember and you went quickly to the window facing the small front garden and drew the curtains. You'd noticed that the family next door walked around rigidly and spoke to their children in really low tones, as if to say, 'this is how you should be behaving too,' and you had noticed that their children would abandon their games and run inside if they saw that any member of your family was coming outside.

Your mother asked why you were late getting home from school and you said, without looking at her, that you had to wait for the drizzle to stop. She responded with a familiar answer, silence.

On the television a man was talking about how the new American President was his relative. Aunty Muna said to your mother that wasn't it interesting that the same people who were quick to claim this black man from America were the same people who said the black girl from London could not be a Rose of Tralee, at which your mother replied, is that so. To which Aunty Muna then wondered aloud why she was even talking about the black girl from London when the African children born in this same country were not even accepted as Irish and do not hold the same passport as other Irish children. She told your mother how once in her daughter's school, all the children's pictures were put up on the wall with their countries of origin written above it and how the children with non-national parents had their parents' countries of origin. She said weren't children of any parentage born in Britain, British or those born in Australia, Australians. You asked her what children born here were called and she said, 'migrant children or children of non-nationals, depending on who their parents were.' She told your mother that she asked her daughter's teacher to change her daughter's country of origin, but the next day, all the pictures were taken down. It was Aunty Muna who had told you not long after you arrived that the people in the Western world liked Africans the way you enjoyed animals in a zoo; you could visit them, feed them, play with them, but they must not be allowed outside their environment.

You sat curled up on the sofa Aunty Muna had been sitting on long after she had gone and you thought of the day you had received the phone call from your mother that her application for family re-unification had been granted and that you would be joining her and your siblings. You had imagined everyone would be like the pen pals your school principal had encouraged your class back home to have. People from Canada, Australia, England and America, that you wrote to unfailingly every Sunday about how hot and dry it was during the Harmattan, the leaves so dry they could cut your fingers quicker and deeper than any knife, and about your French teacher, Mademoiselle Jones, whom you mentioned just because she was the only person you knew who had a foreign name and wore short flowery dresses which made her look all the more exotic. You also tried to impress them with your taste in music and wrote that you liked Usher, Eminem, Britney Spears and Beyoncé, and you were astonished that some of them did not know who they were because they were not into 'that sort of music', and you had wondered what other kind of music there was. You sent them pictures of yourself at home and at school and they sent you their pictures, taken at school and at home. You were so excited to join your mother and had imagined she lived in a big house and drove a big car. Your aunt and your cousins had thought so too because of the money your mother sent every month for your upkeep. In the coming months, you would find out that your mother stacked shelves in a supermarket. She had been a manager at a telecommunications company before she left your father.

She had told you about her friend, Muna. This was at the time when you and she still talked. She said Muna was lucky to have a job in an organisation that looked after the welfare of migrants. Aunty Muna had told her that the organisation had the foresight to employ a migrant as that was the best way to really empower those migrants. She would also tell you other things Aunty Muna had told her; how the other staff in her organisation were polite to her, even though they excluded her in conversations amongst themselves, and *when she made attempts to join in, they would quickly disperse.*

You would find out your sister, who was almost nine, wanted her hair weaved long and flowing down her back and thought Peaches Geldof was cool for walking around barefoot and said she didn't want to visit Africa because Africans were poor and the African children shown on the television had no shoes. You would also find out that your eleven-year-old brother and his friends walked around with their trousers almost at their knees and rapped about everything.

In the college your mother enrolled you in to study travel and tourism, the girls wore a lot of make-up and looked so dark from their tanning, they confused you sometimes. They asked you where you learnt to speak English so well and if it were true Africans lived in trees and how they could never live in a hot country because they would melt. You muttered an empty response, desperate not to show your real emotions, but the sadness would still come when you got home and you would cry into your pillow.

But it was after you met Dermot that you started to write. He came to visit your mother four months after you arrived. He had been working in London for a few months, which was why you had never met him. Your mother introduced him as the nicest Irishman she had ever met. He told you eagerly that he had worked with a lot of charities in Africa and also did some work with Aunty Muna's organisation. He spoke about his experiences through his work with the openness your pen pal letters used to have, which made you like him even though he was old like your mother. And your smile reached your eyes for the first time in a long while because his were not guarded. He told you he hoped to get funding to run a project, helping migrant children and teenagers to integrate through football and dance. When your mother asked him from the kitchen, where she was preparing jollof rice with prawns for him, if one could be taught to integrate, you had jumped in and said you thought it was a great idea. He still responded to your mother's question and said he didn't think there were enough opportunities for people to integrate, to which your mother replied that the church, the school, the road, the shops and the playground should provide enough opportunities for people to integrate if they wanted to. Your mother glimpsed the look of impatience on your face and answered you back with silence.

You could tell him things you could not bring yourself to tell your mother, how you hurried with your shopping because the security men followed you around the shops blatantly and about the man who got on the same bus with you from school, and how he would wave and smile, and you would wave and smile back, until the day he told you he would give you €100 if you slept with him.

You had started with the small things first. And then you started telling him bigger things, about your father and how, in your head, you had blamed your mother for leaving. And how you had always struggled with the anger and guilt but couldn't talk about it because the first time you tried to say something, your mother had stood up from the bed and said, 'It always had to be about you,' and walked out of the room. You told him how for a long time you had felt as if all your family had died when your mother left you behind to travel with your siblings, both of whom were young enough to go with her on her passport. He had nodded his head repeatedly, as if he heard the things you were saying and the ones you left unsaid – that your mother leaving you behind was her way of punishing you.

He took you and your siblings to the cinema and you knew by people's reactions to you that they found it strange, the way their eyes slid away when you caught them looking. The old white couple who mumbled and scowled at him; the black man who looked at you with contempt before turning his back on you, his arms folded across his chest; the young woman with two little children who smiled at you and said too brightly, 'It's lovely today, isn't it?' You wondered if he felt as uncomfortable as you, but you couldn't read his expression. He started a conversation with the young woman but did not include you, so you walked away to look at the sweets until it was time to go in for the movie.

He got the funding for his project and you went with your mother and your nine-year-old sister to watch your eleven-year-old brother play on the migrants' team. There were little groups formed around the pitch; the black group, two white couples that spoke to each other in a foreign language and a large Irish group. Each group mostly ignored the other. When he came around later, he wanted to know if you thought the event was successful, but you dodged the question. You are yet to feel comfortable telling someone something was grand when you didn't think it was.

He told you his dream would be to run more integration football and to go to schools to give anti-racism talks.

You told him then about the little children down the street, of perhaps the ages of five and six, who persistently shouted 'Blackie' at you whenever they saw you walking alone and how their parents talked amongst themselves like they could not hear. He told you not to bother about them. You also told him about the girls in your college who told each other to mind their bags or made so much about their purses being in their bags whenever they wanted to use the toilet. He told you he didn't think the girls meant anything by it. And you wanted to tell him about the woman at church who told you that a Traveller woman had said that Travellers were no longer the lowest class since the arrival of Africans. And you wanted to tell him about the bus driver who dropped you two bus stops away from your stop because there was nobody else apart from you still in the bus. And you wanted to tell him about the man who followed your mother to a supermarket car park and told her that he wanted a BJ, and how your mother told you she had felt bad she didn't have what he wanted until she realised what he meant. You wanted to tell him all these things but you didn't. You cried for a long time on your bed after he left, confused at how alone you felt with so many people around you and the next day, you went into this same Spar shop and bought a diary.

'Thank you,' the leader said, nodding encouragingly when she got to the end. He sifted through the papers in front of him, rearranging them, again and again before glancing around the room. 'So, what does everyone think of the work?'

A was the first to speak. 'I am surprised you wrote in the second person.'

The girl gave A an impassive smile. She wanted to show she could take any criticism.

B tucked her hair behind her ear before speaking. 'I think the story should have a bit of light and shade to it, so that it's not all bleak and negative.'

C – 'I'm not sure what it is, but there is something about writing in the second person that prevents me from caring about the character. I always know I'm reading a work of fiction.'

The leader – 'Why don't you think about breaking it up a little bit? Maybe give us a name somewhere.'

D – 'Why don't we ask her why she used the second person?'

She waited for someone to pose the question but all she saw were expectant eyes raised in her direction. 'I didn't want to personalise it by using a first person and giving the character a particular voice.'

The leader – 'Do you think you can break it up a little bit? Maybe use the second and third person?'

She gave him an 'I'll consider it' nod.

The leader – 'Another thing I would have preferred was for the reader to be the one picking up on the xenophobia like the incident on the bus.'

E – 'I saw it as a kind of paranoia on the part of the character. Like the scene at the cinema where a woman was being nice and she completely misread it.'

'That was exactly where I was going with the story.' The girl turned eagerly to E, glad someone had picked up on it. 'The character's paranoia.'

F – 'My only issue with the story was the lack of narrative thread.'

The comment irritated the girl. Does every story have to have the traditional plot trajectory? The girl wanted to ask F but didn't.

E – 'I think there is a narrative thread – the buying of the diary.'

F – 'I don't think that was enough.'

C – 'I liked the part where she was told by her aunt of how the West perceived Africans.'

A – 'I thought that was a little melodramatic.'

C – 'It might be harsh but the truth usually is.'

The girl nodded repeatedly to show both side of the argument made sense.

G – 'I think you should ground the narration in specific details so we can understand why the girl feels such self-loathing and self-hatred.'

The girl felt a sudden urge to cry, so she scribbled on the paper she had read from, 'self-loathing and self-hatred'.

The leader closed his note book and said, 'OK, that's all for today. Who is presenting next week?'

F raised his hand.

* * *

Later that evening, the girl was alone, considering the story. Although she wanted to keep the second person point of view rather than use it interchangeably with the third person, she still went ahead to make some changes.

It was after meeting Dermot that you started to write. He came to visit your mother four months after you arrived. He had been working in London which was why you had never met him. Your mother introduced him to you by saying, 'Didi, meet the nicest Irishman I have ever met.'

You felt an ache around your heart as you remembered the reasons you were mad at him, so you tried to reason out his point of view in your head. Your classmates who asked their friends to mind their bags were actually not doing anything wrong; the bus driver who dropped you two stops away from your bus stop could have done so be due to road works; the man in the supermarket who asked your mother for a BJ is just sick; and the children who called out 'Blackie' at you whenever they saw you passing could just be what they were, children.

She emailed the changes to the others and it wasn't long before she started to get their comments back.

B – 'I'm happy you kept the 'you' voice, which really highlighted her anonymity. Please don't change it. I did think it could be useful to still temper the racism she experienced with examples of kind behaviour too. In places there is so much bias, so much prejudice, that it almost swallows itself.'

F – 'If you can structure this piece around some kind of cohesive event or a series of events beyond buying the diary itself, the writing will really stand out.'

D – 'Very strong. Admired your use of the second person. It worked very well. Clear straightforward narrative line. Work on the bleak picture. How you would do this, I don't know.'

A – 'I'm so glad you wrote this. I found it believable! You'll hate this suggestion, but … I'd actually be interested in seeing this rewritten in chronological order with the girl given a name.'

E – 'You are able to talk about difficult material without laying a heavy layer of judgment over everything. Also, I really think that the second person is powerful. I wouldn't change it.'

She dreaded G's response the most. She took her time to open it. 'Full of great details, but I would like you to a) lose the second person and b) observe chronology.'

C did not reply.

THE EGG BROKE

With the last of the tiny pebbles I had gathered from the Iyi Ekulu, I secured the edge of my dripping wrapper. I had it spread out on the thatched roof of the hut I shared with my husband, Ugo, and our two-year-old daughter, Chika. The roof was low enough for me to reach just by standing on my toes.

'*Nwunye anyi!*' My father-in-law, Nwigwe, called out to me on his way to his hut. 'Please do not overwork yourself or people will start saying that we don't take good care of you, especially in your condition!'

'Papa,' laughing I turned to him, 'how am I overworking myself now, hmm? I'm only pregnant, not sick. Besides, have you forgotten that I've done it before?'

'This one is different oh! This is our *idi okpara*, so please handle with care,' he retorted, adjusting his wrapper.

I could tell he was enjoying himself. I knew he meant no harm and that he genuinely adores Chika, his only grandchild. But I knew he would have been happier if I had given Ugo a male child first, as that would have given him more honour amongst his kinsmen, and assured them that he now has someone who will inherit their farmland, for Chika, as a girl, will not be left her father's land as that is an abomination in Ugwuoba.

'Eeh! *Ngwanu*, I'll go and tell Chika you said she's not important,' I said, turning as if to go inside the hut where Chika was sleeping.

'Hei! *Biko*! Let me run before this woman puts words into my mouth that I did not say.' He turned and quickly limped into his hut as I laughed after him.

I love being a part of this family. Most women in my shoes would have been threatened by their husband's family that they would be returned to their parents for being unsatisfactory. After all, Mgbeke was sent back to her parents by her mother-in-law immediately after she had her daughter. But all Ugo and his parents do is constantly reassure me that they do not care and will love any child I bring into their family. I pray every day to Nne Iyi, our river goddess, for a son this time. Nnebu, my mother-in-law has only two sons, Ugo and his younger brother, Izuchukwu, and for now, she is very supportive of me. Another daughter for Ugo might change her or Ugo for he might be mocked by his friends and possibly some of his kinsmen. Only Nne Iyi knows what that might push him to do.

I swallowed a sigh as I poured out the remaining water in my clay pot and placed it on my head. Deep in thought, I did not see the firewood that Izuchukwu had gathered earlier in the day and dumped carelessly on the tiny path to my hut until my left toe hit a log.

'Ewoooo!' I yelped in pain, hopping on one leg. I danced around holding the clay pot on my head with one hand while trying to cradle my toe with the other, confused by the pain.

'*O gini* Ogechi? Ogechi! Ogechi!'

Nnebu screamed, running out of her hut to me.

'What is it?' she asked, coming closer. She took the empty pot off my head and put it on the ground. 'Save the important one first,' she scolded, pointing at my protruding stomach.

'What happened?' she asked again.

I told my mother-in-law how I had missed seeing the firewood on the path in time. Nnebu released a series of curses on her son, Izuchukwu.

'I don't understand that boy. Every day, I ask Nne Iyi how could she give me a son as lazy as him!'

Nnebu bent and lifted my leg to take a closer look at the toe. Immediately she let it go and straightened herself. I let out another scream and reached to hold her arm to stop myself from falling.

'Oge,' she whispered, her voice terrified. 'It's your left leg.'

'Eh?' I said, holding onto her. 'It's your left leg,' she repeated, taking my hand away from her arm slowly as she moved away from me, pointing at my leg.

It was then the realisation came and it made me angry that she was thinking of such superstitious nonsense when I was in such discomfort.

'*Ngwa*,' she ordered, 'pray to Nne Iyi quickly. You shouldn't waste time with such things,' she snapped.

I moved my aching leg to the back of my right leg, dutifully, muttering the prayer. 'My bad leg go to my back, my right leg come forward, and let us go. All the bad things that went forward when I put out my left leg first, Nne Iyi, please take them away.'

Nnebu bent again to have a look at my toe without touching it. She told me to go into my hut and lie down, standing back from me as she spoke, as if she was afraid to touch me. A few minutes later she came in to me, carrying my sleeping daughter Chika in one arm and a paste she had made from the healing bitter-leaf plant, Onugbu. She put Chika on the bed beside me and Chika squeezed her face to cry.

'Shh …' I said softly, rubbing her back gently until she went back to sleep.

Nnebu came and knelt by the end of my mud bed. She applied the paste to my toe, telling me it would stop the toe from swelling. She reminded me to continue to pray to Nne Iyi to avert any evil plan of the enemy that made me stub my left toe.

'Try and sleep. It will help the pain,' she said on her way out, and I heard the mat curtain drop back into place with a sound that made Chika stir in her sleep.

I shifted my body closer to the warmth of my daughter, holding back tears from the throbbing in my toe. With the pain came the fear and anxiety I had been trying to keep away in the past weeks. I moved back a little from Chika's body to place a shaking hand on my heavy stomach. It was a few seconds before I felt it. I took my hand off quickly. Terrified of the weight and of what I had felt.

'Every pregnancy is different,' I said out loud.

There was no doubt that this pregnancy felt completely different. I knew what I was doing was a poor attempt to calm myself and not give into the fear that was growing inside me. It was time to go to Umuochi and see my mother. I needed to confide in someone. As much as Nnebu was a wonderful woman, the enormity of the secret I could be carrying might destroy her. I closed my eyes and wished for rest, singing a childhood lullaby quietly. But my late father's voice kept forcing its way into my head. 'When that which is greater than a child happens, the child goes looking for its mother,' he would say with a smile as he took us to our mother after we had a fall. Or was he looking grave? But why would he be sad? Did he already know that his muddy footprints would soon be missing from the path that leads into my mother's hut?

* * *

When I neared my father's compound, a loud chorus of greetings came from the distance. One of my nephews had spotted me from his perch on top of a palmwine tree.

'*Da* Ogechi *alota o yo yo*! *Da* Ogechi *alota o yo yo*!'

He was soon joined by his three siblings and my other cousins. They sang as they led me, bags and all, towards my mother's hut, fallen guava leaves stopping dust from gathering behind us. My mother, on hearing the commotion, ran out of the hut that is used as a communal kitchen, to see truly if it was me.

'Ogechi!' she said, pulling me to her. 'Is everything OK?' She stepped back to study me. 'You didn't send any message to say you were coming. Did you travel down all by yourself in this condition? Where is Ugo? How is Chika? Are you and your husband living in peace?'

'*Mma biko,*' I laughed in exasperation when she paused to catch her breath. '*I ga ajugbu kwam.* Do you want to kill me with all these questions?'

I gave the children the *ihe ahia* I came with; boiled groundnuts to share amongst themselves and dry cassava slices for their parents. They dispersed happily with loud calls of '*Da daru*' ringing out in the evening air around them.

* * *

It was late in the evening. Everywhere was quiet except for the noise of the crickets. The children had been sent into their parents' huts to sleep. My four brothers, their wives, and some of our neighbouring kinsmen had moved to the back of the huts to play. The younger men were already wrestling under the watchful eyes of the older men. The women were plaiting each other's hair and gossiping about things that happened at the market or on their way to the stream. My mother and I sat shoulder to shoulder outside her hut. The cooking fire had been put out, but the smell of firewood still filled the air. With the moon not full, and the stars only providing a sliver of light, I could only make out a little of my mother's face.

'*O gini* Ogechi? I can tell that your heart is heavy.'

Throughout the evening, I could feel that she had been watching me. She would stop in the middle of her cooking to study me. And a few times, our eyes had met.

'Mma I'm fine,' I felt a need to say.

'What of Ugo?' she quickly asked.

'All is well between us,' I replied. 'I missed you, that's all.'

She nodded her head slowly, not accepting my words but careful not to push.

'I can tell that all is not well with you,' she said again.

'Mma, I think I'm pregnant with twins,' I blurted out. My plans of how I would gently tell her starting with the whispered suspicion of the midwife, Ucheego, and the symptoms I had been experiencing were totally forgotten.

'God forbid!' Mma said, jumping up and covering my mouth with her palm. How she was able to make out my mouth in the darkness, only Nne Iyi knows.

'Shhh! *Mechi onu gi*! Shut up your mouth! How can you utter such abomination or even think it in your head?' She took her hand off my mouth to push my head back. Her voice rose as she continued talking. 'Do you even know what you are saying?'

'Mma, please, someone might come out,' I begged her. I waited for her to sit down before continuing. 'I have only been pregnant for just twenty market days. Did you see how heavy I looked?'

'Pregnancies are different, that's why. You are carrying a son for your husband.' She said the last part forcefully, as if to say that is how I should have been thinking.

'That's not all, Mma. A few weeks ago, I was cracking some palm nuts and not one but *two* came out. It turned out to be *ejima*, twins! The she-goat that Nnebu gave to me when I had Chika, has just given birth to twins. My hen laid only two eggs two market days ago. Everything around me is happening in twos. I have hit my left toe twice these past few days ...'

'Have you gone mad? What is all this nonsense, Ogechi? Has the pregnancy affected your brain?' Mma shouted at me again. She leaned her head to peer at me in the darkness.

'Mma, I can even feel two heartbeats,' I said, my voice wobbling, 'Ucheego, the midwife felt them first.'

At that, Mma jumped off her stool. I heard a clattering sound as the stool rolled on the ground before stopping.

'Ogechi oo! Ogechi o! Ogechi oo!' Mma clutched my head as she cried out my name repeatedly. It was a gut-wrenching cry. I wiped the tears from my cheeks.

'Mma, who have I wronged? What did I do to deserve this? What did I do to bring this upon myself, Mma?'

* * *

I lie on my bed pretending not to be awake as I secretly watch Ugo get ready to go out. He has to tap his palmwine before daybreak to get the best tasting wine for sale. Facing Ugo and his family has become a chore that I leave as long as I possibly can each morning. There have been a lot of changes since my return from Umuochi.

Mma advised me to tell Ugo and his family about my suspicions. It feels like forever since I did that. The heaviness I used to feel between my breasts has come over all of us. Ugo has aged before my eyes. My Ugo, whose footsteps could be heard long before his shadow fell on the footpath now walks as if he is afraid the ground will open up suddenly and swallow him. His usual joviality is now a thing of the past.

Nnebu now drags herself around with stooped shoulders. Most of the work around the house has fallen to her – looking after Chika, cooking for Nwigwe, Izuchukwu, Ugo and myself – as I am too heavy to help and cannot even lie on my mud bed without her and Ugo there to help lift my legs. Not only that, she also looks after her husband, Nwigwe, who is now bedridden from a mysterious sickness despite visits from the best medicine men in Ugwuoba. She refuses every offer of help from their relatives, and I suspect it is because she's scared of people finding out that I am carrying twins.

* * *

I was still lying on the bed, staring into the dark room when Nnebu came into my hut. Ugo had taken the *mpata* with him to light his way into the forest where Nwigwe's portion of land is. She nudged my knees with her hands and helped me to move to make room on the mud bed for her to sit.

'We need to talk,' she said, taking my hands in hers. '*Nwunye anyi*, I think the time has come for us to prepare ourselves.'

My body stiffened in rejection. There was no light in the room, so Nnebu must have felt my withdrawal for she quickly placed her hand on top of my hand which was on my stomach and held it.

'As soon as the twins are delivered, Akuiwu, the Chief Priest will come to take them away. A lot of rituals and cleansing will need to be performed. The gods need to be appeased. They might be taken to Agu Iyi. I don't know these things very well …'

'They – them, they – them.' I could no longer contain the pain of the last few months. 'Is it my sons you are talking about, Nnebu? Do you know I have named them? I feel them all the time, you know. I know when they are sleeping and when they are moving. They know my voice and they listen to me when I am singing to them.'

I waited for Nnebu to speak and when she didn't, I continued. 'Why are they even evil, Nnebu? Do you know?'

'Erm, I think our ancestors … our people think …' Nnebu's voice trailed off.

'You don't even know,' I said, my voice rising, sounding cruel even to my own ears. 'You don't even know why they are evil,' I repeated. 'Maybe we will be outcasts in Ugwuoba for something you don't even have an answer for,' I yelled.

My eyes fixed on her dim figure in the darkness as I continued to scream, even though I knew she had no control over anything. There was only silence from Nnebu's corner. My rage left me as quickly as it came. It was as if I needed to say those things out loud to someone. I felt for Nnebu's hands again.

'Nne, I'm scared.'

'I know,' she said as I felt her hand on my face, her rough thumb rubbing off a trail of my tear.

* * *

The two days I was in labour and the period after the birth has remained like a morning fog in harmattan. I have tried so hard to remember things in the sequence in which they happened, but I can't. I can only recollect in fragments. I saw the faces of the men that took my sons, Chukwuemeka and Chukwuma away; faces painted white and eyes that were hard and vacant. The six men each had palm twigs to ward off evil forces clasped in their mouths. Their white cloth wrappers were tied around them like they were going to a wrestling match.

I still see the red-eyed faces of Ugo, Izuchukwu, Mma and Nnebu as they looked on. They now walk around with shoulders bent from helplessness and shame. I hope their shame is for themselves; for who would not raise a finger to save their own? My heart has since hardened against each one of them.

I remember watching the Chief Priest invoking the gods of Ugwuoba before he walked out of my hut backwards, a string of incantations called out at each footstep. At his command, his high priests had carried my sons away. Yes, I still see these things. Maybe not in the right order, but I see them with these eyes that have known no sleep since it all happened. And I have carried the weight of my visions and the weight of my hatred around wherever I go.

It is now two market weeks since their birth, eight days since my sons were snatched away from me and not a single tear has dropped from these eyes of mine. I have travelled the length and width of Ugwuoba looking for them. I have entered places where women do not go, and I have entered places where humans do not go. I have walked fearlessly through great forests, crossed deep rivers and marched into sacred places, my breasts heavy with milk and a mix of their blood and mine dripping down my legs.

Neighbours have stopped me to offer empty words of kindness. 'Ogechi, my daughter, the *ajo Iyi* that gave you those twins has been defeated.'

Friends have passed on meaningless words of wisdom. 'Don't ever go to the stream to bathe at night. That is how you get these twins inside your body.'

Kinsmen have given unsolicited advice. 'Before you eat any meal, throw some on the floor and ask all the twins in the evil forest to come and eat their own so they won't try to enter your body just so they can taste your delicious cooking.'

Ugo and Nnebu have told me my search is a waste of time. Ugo said in time we will have more children. I have listened and stared back wordlessly. I have refused to live with hope. It's for people who have fear.

I have called on every god in Ugwuoba. I have knocked on every door. I will search more forests, and swim across more rivers. I will even try the strangers' religion if it will bring back my sons. I have four more days before they will be buried alive and these eyes will know no rest until I find my sons.

Ireland: Asylum Seekers and Refugees

by Liam Thornton

On Ireland and migration

Far from the land of one hundred thousand welcomes, Melatu Uche Okorie's work shines a light onto issues that for far too long have been swept under the carpet. Irish society's ability to condemn, institutionalise, and castigate persons due to differences is ever present in 2018. Ireland for generations has been a country of emigration. The experience of the emigrant has been told in word and verse; the mythical Irish emigrant pining for home, or getting along with life in their new-found land or mapping the struggles and adversities the person succumbed to or overcame. Ireland did not experience any post-World War II inward migration. It was only during the 1990s that any appreciable number of migrants came to Ireland. This question of 'who belongs' has been an underlying current of debate within Irish society. This was most startlingly confronted in the 2004 Citizenship Referendum. Melatu's characters in 'Under the Awning' discuss these questions of belonging, asking are children born in Britain, British, children born in Australia, Australians, children born in Ireland, Irish. Yet, in law the answer to this for transnational families is often no – these children are not citizens of where they are born or where they belong. The Referendum saw the right of all children to Irish citizenship where born on the island of Ireland withdrawn. The referendum campaign took place in a sea of hostility, where the Irish state was seen as under an existential threat, with 'illegal' crossings via the birth canal viewed as an issue of significant public comment and decision. This feeling of not belonging, of being an outsider, of challenging or accepting the status quo is threaded throughout Melatu's work. This piece seeks to provide some political and legal context to issues that arise from some of Melatu's stories, to provide some sense of understanding of the quagmires that arise when seeking protection in a land far from home.

On asylum and protection

We do not know what happened to the protagonist or her twins in 'The Egg Broke'. The story raises significant and important questions about the right to seek asylum. Would the protagonist, if she managed to escape from her country, with or without her children, be entitled to refugee protection in another State? The custom of seeking asylum or refuge from harm is ancient. Stories traverse all the major religions about their prophets fleeing their homelands and having to find sanctuary elsewhere. Within the international community, there is only a limited degree of human rights protection for persons fleeing. To be recognised as a refugee, a person must be outside her country of origin and not want to return to her country of origin as she has a real risk of being persecuted if she does return. The reasons for the real risk of being persecuted must relate to the person's race, religion, nationality, membership of a particular social group and/or political opinion. Refugee status is a limited status. As well as showing that a person cannot return to their country of origin, a person will have to show that the harm she faces is 'country-wide'. If there is an area within her own State in which a person can, without too much difficulty, reside away from the persecution that they fear, then that person is not, *in law*, a refugee. Refugee status only comes about if the persecution feared is conducted by, or with the acquiescence, of a State and must be country-wide. Where the State is the persecutor, then the requirement that the person has a real risk of being persecuted can be seen as country-wide. However, where it is private individuals or communities that cause the persecution, then it may be that the person should move elsewhere in the State to escape this persecution, even where the person may not have any familial or social ties with that region of the country. The international community has only committed to protecting a small subset of individuals who face denial of their human rights. As the (now) President of the Supreme Court of the

United Kingdom, Baroness Brenda Hale, noted in a 2007 decision:

Very bad things happen to a great many people but the international community has not committed itself to giving them all a safe haven.

This does not seek to take away from the other harms or human rights abuses that people may face, but it does emphasise the fact that State protection is not absolute.

There has been some recognition of the difficulties people may face in coming within the strict definition of refugee. Therefore, under EU law, another protection status exists – subsidiary protection. Irish law provides that where a non-EU citizen or a stateless person does not qualify for refugee status, but there are substantial grounds for believing that the person, if returned to her country of origin, would face a 'real risk' of 'serious harm' she will be entitled to subsidiary protection. Serious harm is defined as the death penalty or execution, torture or inhuman or degrading treatment or punishment, and a serious and individual threat to a civilian's life or person by reason of indiscriminate violence in situations of international or internal armed conflict.

Like refugee status, subsidiary protection does not protect against all types of serious harm, but only harm of a particular quality or character. There have been some interesting judicial decisions on what might constitute serious harm, such as being subject to poverty and/or a wholly inadequate health care system might be seen as inhuman and degrading. In the Court of Justice of the European Union case of *M'Bodj v Etat Belge*, a Mauritian national argued that he was entitled to subsidiary protection where the risk of 'serious harm' emerged from a lack of even the most basic health care to deal with a health condition. The European Court determined that the concept of serious harm cannot include harms emerging due to poor health care within a person's country of origin.

Fairness and the length of time decisions take is something that has been a central feature of political and legal discussions in Ireland over the last twenty years. Throughout this time, various Ministers for Justice have promised that the system was always just one reform away from ensuring decisions were reached in a time-frame of between ten weeks and nine months. In 2005, the then Minister for Justice, Michael McDowell, stated before the Oireachtas Justice Committee:

> *I'm making it very clear that you will be going home within 10 weeks of making a claim in Ireland, and I would much prefer to have a system where I could have an interview at the airport, find out the cock and bull stories that are going on and put them on the next flight. But unfortunately the UN Convention requires me to go through due process in respect of all these claims.*

Due process and providing a person with a fair hearing to determine their protection claim was viewed as nothing more than an inconvenience. In 2006, two members of the then Refugee Appeals Tribunal resigned in protest of what they saw as unfair allocation of refugee cases to those Tribunal Members who were more likely to affirm the negative decision of the Office of the Refugee Applications Commissioner. For many years, Ireland had one of the lowest recognition rates of refugees in the European Union. The then Secretary General of the

Department of Justice, Mr. Sean Aylward, stated the following before the UN Committee Against Torture in 2011:

In terms of delays in processing asylum applications, a great deal of the time it was in the best interest of the applicant to drag out the process and delay it and their lawyers used every conceivable human contrivance to delay and defer the outcome when the application was manifestly incorrect and ill-founded. It had almost become a legal racket to string out the process of these applications and it undermined the credibility of the State and its processes.

In 2012, the Irish Refugee Council conducted a study on the low recognition rate of protection claims in Ireland, concluding that:

There is a culture of disbelief that itself informs the approach that some Tribunal Members take and the way in which they set about the task of deciding the appeals.

As of December 2017, the waiting time for an asylum seeker to have her interview before the International Protection Office is 20 months and rising. This will have knock-on effects on the appeals body, the

International Protection Appeals Tribunal. It takes time for a decision to emerge as to whether a person is a refugee or in need of subsidiary protection. The waiting for papers, for recognition or rejection comes to the fore in 'This Hostel Life'. Having decisions made about you by another person is something many of us can relate to. However, only in rare circumstances will such decisions potentially involve life or death. Therefore, the operation of decision-makers within the International Protection Office and the International Protection Appeals Tribunal should be beyond reproach. There should be either a strong yes, that this person is entitled to protection in Ireland, or a strong no, this person is not entitled to protection in Ireland. This waiting will often take place in a system known as 'direct provision'.

On direct provision

One of the first documents given to asylum seekers in Ireland who enter direct provision is the Reception and Integration Agency's *House Rules* for accommodation centres. The House Rules proclaim that the direct provision centre 'is your home while

your application for protection is being processed.'
'Home' is an interesting concept as, within law, the
protection of an individual or families 'home' is a
central concern. The right to respect for one's home
is an underlying theme of all core international and
European human rights instruments. Article 40.5.
of the Irish Constitution states that:

> *The dwelling of every citizen is inviolable and*
> *shall not be forcibly entered save in accordance*
> *with law.*

This applies to citizens and non-citizens. The concept
of this protection of the dwelling or the 'home' has
been used by Irish courts to strike down certain
house rules that the Reception and Integration
Agency implemented in direct provision centres.
Yet, in 'This Hostel Life' we are immediately drawn
into the mundane, the everyday, but also something
quite alien – the fact that direct provision does not
seem to be like a home. Waiting. Lots of waiting.
Waiting for a decision. Waiting to be provided with
basic provisions for living. Waiting for somebody
to tell you when you can eat, and what you can
eat. Subject to the whims of 'the manager'. 'This
Hostel Life' provides such a troubling picture of

how Ireland treats asylum seekers. Direct provision includes accommodation and the provision of either meals or, more unusually, the ability for a person to cook their own meals with ingredients provided by the direct provision accommodation centre. Direct provision is also used in a short-hand manner to describe the rights and services all asylum seekers in Ireland should be guaranteed. This includes a weekly payment of €21.60 per adult and per child, the right of children to an education, at least up until completion of the Leaving Certificate and the medical card that asylum seekers are provided allowing them access to healthcare free of charge on the same basis as Irish citizens and other residents who have a medical card. Asylum seekers cannot access most other social welfare payments, nor (until recently) could seek or enter employment, nor can asylum seekers travel outside of the State, without the consent of the Minister for Justice and Equality.

There was a time before direct provision, a time when need was catered for through the general social welfare system. So, for a period of time, it was thought that the general welfare system could cater for asylum seekers. Asylum seekers would receive supplementary welfare allowance if they met conditions for this payment, or one-parent family payment if the person was a single parent, or non-contributory old-age pension if the asylum seeker was over 65. In March 1998, the then Minister for Justice in Ireland, John O'Donoghue T.D., proclaimed:

> *It is a source of puzzlement to many people that at a time when there are no conflicts taking place near our borders ... when we have no colonial links with countries in which political turmoil is taking place and when the number of claims for refugee status is declining in other European states, the Irish state shows a major increase.*

In introducing direct provision, John O'Donoghue gave assurances that direct provision was a time limited system which, in the normal course of events, would end within six months after an asylum seeker's protection claim was determined. In fact, in its early years of existence, up until about 2003, stories abound about how particular Community Welfare Officers would grant asylum seekers rent allowance and access to the full rate of supplementary welfare allowance payments so that they could move out of direct provision. This practice was stopped in its tracks by a change in the law in 2003. From its very foundation, serious concerns were raised about the alien nature of the system of direct provision. In *Beyond the Pale*, Dr Angela Veale and Professor Brian Fanning explored the impact of the system of direct provision on the rights of children. This 2001 report noted the significant level of social control over asylum seekers lives, the condemnation of children to poverty by design, and the highly institutionalised nature of the system of direct provision.

Yet, in Ireland this system of direct provision accommodation centres and near cashless living grew roots. Now standing at 32 accommodation centres across Ireland, the direct provision system seems like it is here to stay. Since 1997, governments of different hues, Fianna Fail-Progressive Democrats, Fianna Fail-Green, Fine Gael-Labour, Fine Gael-Independents have all made similar pronouncements, about how just a few more changes were needed before all asylum seekers would have a decision on their protection claim within six to nine months. Political parties that ferociously opposed the system of direct provision while in opposition, happily lived with, and often defended, the system of direct provision once they had reached the dizzying heights of governmental office. Throughout the last 18 years, platitudes from various politicians abound. So, in 2018, Ireland excludes asylum seekers to accommodation centres, away and apart from Irish society. That such a situation may last for many years, with years of queuing for food, a miserly €21.60 per week and highly institutionalised hostel living speaks volumes about how Irish society protects the weakest.

The system of direct provision is a system of enforced poverty, the core purpose of which is to make Ireland a deeply unattractive location for asylum seekers to have their protection claim determined. In 2015, a group composed of a chairperson, Dr Bryan McMahon, civil society organisations, one asylum seeker and representatives of government departments were tasked with, amongst other things, suggesting improvements to the system of direct provision. The McMahon Report made a significant number of recommendations about making the system of direct provision more bearable for those subjected to it such as the ability for asylum seekers to cook their own food and an increase in the direct provision allowance. Some of these recommendations have been implemented, many more have yet to be implemented. The McMahon Report could not suggest alternatives to the system of direct provision in Ireland, as its terms of reference were restricted to considering improvements to the existing system.

Only recently has the absolute nature of this enforced poverty been challenged, with the partial relaxation on asylum seekers working. The rationale for prohibiting asylum seekers from working between 1996 and 2018 boiled down to two core reasons. First, it may attract more asylum seekers from other countries if Ireland were to allow asylum seekers to work. Second, the shared border with the North of Ireland and wanting to ensure that the 'common travel area' would not be 'abused' by those who did not hold Irish or British citizenship. A decision of the Supreme Court finally ended the absolute prohibition barring asylum seekers from working. In November 2017, in response to the judgment, the Government indicated that Ireland would agree to be bound by the EU Reception Directive on the rights of asylum seekers. Until such time as EU law applies, asylum seekers in Ireland can only enter employment where the position pays over €30,000 per annum. There is an extensive list of prohibited employment areas, mainly in the hospitality, retail and social care sectors. If these restrictions were not enough, an asylum seeker or her potential employer will have to pay €1,000 for a 12-month work permit. Additionally, an asylum seeker must have a passport to apply for the work permit. Given that asylum seekers can often only access Ireland by travelling on false identity documents, many asylum seekers will not be able to meet this condition.

Over 5,000 men, women and children remain in direct provision centres today. Convicted of no crime, the system of enforced dependency and institutionalisation reminds me of the crueller and less understanding Ireland of the borstal, the Magdalene laundry, the mother and baby home, the mental institution. Using the law and appeals of human rights will not fundamentally change the degrading nature of direct provision. Only by engaging with the political sphere, by telling our elected representatives that direct provision is simply not acceptable, can we hope to see this system abolished.

Dr Liam Thornton is an assistant professor in law in the School of Law, University College Dublin. Liam regularly blogs on issues of human rights law in Ireland at www.liamthornton.ie.

BIBLIOGRAPHY

Case C-542/13, *M'Bodj v Etat Belge*, decision of
the Court of Justice of the European Union
(Grand Chamber, 18 December 2014).

Coulter, C. 'Looking for fairness and consistency
in a secretive refugee appeals system', *The Irish
Times*, 06 June 2005.

Coulter, C. 'Bias claim against member of refugee
appeal tribunal', *The Irish Times*, 31 March
2006.

Coulter, C. 'Strife proceeded refugee body's
demise', *The Irish Times*, 20 September 2006.

Egan, S. 'The Refugee Definition in Irish Law' in
Suzanne Egan (ed.) *International Human Rights:*

Perspectives from Ireland (Bloomsbury: Dublin, 2015).

Fanning, B. *Racism and Social Change in the Republic of Ireland* (Manchester University Press: Dublin, 2002).

Gilmartin, M. *Ireland and Migration in the 21ˢᵗ Century* (Manchester University Press: Dublin, 2015).

Fornah v Secretary of State for the Home Department [2007] 1 AC 412.

Irish Refugee Council, *Difficult to Believe: The Assessment of Asylum Claims in Ireland* (IRC: Dublin, 2012).

Lentin, R. 'Ireland: Racial State and Crisis Racism' (2007) 30(4) *Ethnic and Racial Studies Review* 610.

Luangrath, N. 'No Date on the Door: Direct Provision Housing, Child Asylum Seekers, and Ireland's Violations of the United Nations Convention on the Rights of the Child' in

Ensor M., Goździak E. (eds) *Children and Forced Migration* (Palgrave Macmillan, 2016).

McMahon Report, *Working Group to Report to Government on Improvements to the Protection Process, including Direct Provision and Supports to Asylum Seekers* (June 2015).

Mullally, S. 'Citizenship and Family Life in Ireland: Asking the Question "Who Belongs"' (2005) 25 (4) *Legal Studies* 578.

Nasc, *Working Paper on Government's Progress on McMahon Report*, December 2017.

Refugee Act 1996 (as amended).

Thornton, L. 'The Rights of Others: Asylum Seekers and Direct Provision in Ireland' (2014) 3(2) *Irish Community Development Law Journal* 22.

Thornton, L. 'A Preliminary Analysis of the Working Group Report and Recommendations on Direct Provision' (30 June 2015).

Thornton, L. 'Justice pays lip service to asylum seekers' work rights' *The Irish Times*, 25 January 2018.

UNHCR, *Handbook on Procedures and Criteria for Determining Refugee Status* (2011 edn, as revised).

About the Author

Born in Nigeria, Melatu Uche Okorie came to Ireland in 2006. It was during her eight and a half years living in the direct provision system that she began to write.

She has an M. Phil. in Creative Writing from Trinity College, Dublin and her writing has been published in several anthologies. In 2008, she won the Metro Éireann writing award for her story 'Gathering Thoughts'. Melatu has a strong interest in the rights of asylum seekers and migrant education in Ireland and is working on a PhD in Trinity College, Dublin focused on creative writing centres as nurturing grounds for creativity.

This Hostel Life is her first book.

About Skein Press

Skein Press was established in June, 2017. One of our goals is to amplify the voices of writers from an ethnic minority background, which are largely absent from Irish literature at the moment. We also hope to foster fresh and thought-provoking writing featuring perspectives not often represented in Irish literature.

www.skeinpress.com
skeinpress@gmail.com